# The Day Jimmy's Boa Ate the Wash

TOPIC NUMBER ONE
CORN
NOTE: THERE WILL BE A QUIZ WHEN WE RETURN TO CLASS.
UNDERSTANDING CORN & POULTRY
CORN for KIDS
VOLUME X
THE YOUNG PERSON'S GUIDE TO POULTRY
FARM GUIDE
CORN

# The Day Jimmy's Boa Ate the Wash

*by* TRINKA HAKES NOBLE
*pictures by* STEVEN KELLOGG

PUFFIN BOOKS

PUFFIN BOOKS
Published by the Penguin Group
Penguin Putnam Books for Young Readers,
345 Hudson Street, New York, New York 10014, U.S.A.
Penguin Books Ltd, 80 Strand, London WC2R ORL, England
Penguin Books Australia Ltd, Ringwood, Victoria, Australia
Penguin Books Canada Ltd, 10 Alcorn Avenue, Toronto, Ontario, Canada M4V 3B2
Penguin Books (N.Z.) Ltd, 182-190 Wairau Road, Auckland 10, New Zealand
Penguin Books Ltd, Registered Offices: Harmondsworth, Middlesex, England


Library of Congress Catalog Card Number: 80-15098
Printed in the United States of America
First Pied Piper Printing 1984
C O B E

43 45 47 49 50 48 46 44 42
A Pied Piper Book is a registered trademark of
Dial Books for Young Readers,
a division of Penguin Books USA Inc.,
® TM 1,163,686 and ® TM 1,054,312.

THE DAY JIMMY'S BOA ATE THE WASH
is published in a hardcover edition by
Dial Books for Young Readers.
ISBN 0-14-054623-5

The full-color artwork was prepared
using ink and pencil line and watercolor washes.
It was then camera-separated and reproduced
as red, blue, yellow, and black halftones.

For Sandy and Randon,
my very best friends

T. H. N.

For Melanie and Tom,
with love

S. K.

"How was your class trip to the farm?"

"Oh...boring...kind of dull...until the cow started crying."

"A cow...crying?"
"Yeah, you see, a haystack fell on her."

“But a haystack doesn’t just fall over.”

"It does if a farmer crashes into it with his tractor."
"Oh, come on, a farmer wouldn't do that."

"He would if he were too busy yelling at the pigs to get off our school bus."

"What were the pigs doing on the bus?"

"Eating our lunches."

"Why were they eating your lunches?"
"Because we threw their corn at each other, and they didn't have anything else to eat."

"Well, that makes sense, but why were you throwing corn?"

"Because we ran out of eggs."

"Out of eggs? Why were you throwing eggs?"

"Because of the boa constrictor."

"THE BOA CONSTRICTOR!"

"Yeah, Jimmy's pet boa constrictor."

"What was Jimmy's pet boa constrictor doing on the farm?"
"Oh, he brought it to meet all the farm animals,
but the chickens didn't like it."

"You mean he took it into the hen house?"

"Yeah, and the chickens started squawking and flying around."

"Go on, go on. What happened?"

"Well, one hen got excited and laid an egg, and it landed on Jenny's head."

"The hen?"

"No, the egg. And it broke—yucky—all over her hair."

"What did she do?"

"She got mad because she thought Tommy threw it, so she threw one at him."

"What did Tommy do?"

"Oh, he ducked and the egg hit Marianne in the face.

“So she threw one at Jenny but she missed and hit Jimmy,
who dropped his boa constrictor.”

"Oh, I know, and the next thing you knew, everyone was throwing eggs, right?"

"Right."

"And when you ran out of eggs, you threw the pigs' corn, right?"

"Right again."

"Well, what finally stopped it?"

"Well, we heard the farmer's wife screaming."

"Why was she screaming?"

“We never found out, because Mrs. Stanley made us get on the bus, and we sort of left in a hurry without the boa constrictor.”

"I bet Jimmy was sad because he left his pet boa constrictor."

"Oh, not really. We left in such a hurry that one of the pigs didn't get off the bus, so now he's got a pet pig."

"Boy, that sure sounds like an exciting trip."
"Yeah, I suppose, if you're the kind of kid who likes class trips to the farm."

GRAND PRIX

our
BOA